This Book Belongs To:
_____

For Candy, my childhood Irish Setter, whose paws left permanent prints on my heart—and for our little Oatmeal.

Author: Amy Skala Tischmann
Illustrator: Eduardo Paj

Love, Pal (First Edition)
Red Birds Publishing, LLC Text and Illustrations Copyright @ 2025.
All Rights Reserved

No part of this publication or the characters within it, may be reproduced, printed, distributed or transmitted in any form, or by any means, including photocopying, recording or other electronic, or any mechanical methods without prior written permission from the publisher.

Library of Congress Control Number: 2025905710

ISBN: 978-1-7367356-6-4
Red Birds Publishing, LLC offers wholesale discounts.
For more information, please contact
the website: www.redbirdspublishing.com

Printed in China

Love, Pal

Amy Skala Tischmann
Eduardo Paj

I've been busy in Heaven, enjoying new friends,
some are dogs, some are squirrels—and the fun never ends.

There are dog parks and toys and unlimited bones,
and the best doggy ice cream with *Huge* waffle cones.

We never need haircuts, our fur's always groomed,
and treats are so tasty, they're quickly consumed.

We find bags of beef jerky and rabbits to chase,
and belly rubs spark sweet dreams of your face.

We ride in the car with windows rolled down—
the breeze in our fur as we cruise through the town.

There are fancy bandanas in every fine print,
some are silky, some checkered, and some come in mint.

I've even made friends with a jovial cat,
and he'll always play chase—oh, I sure do love that!

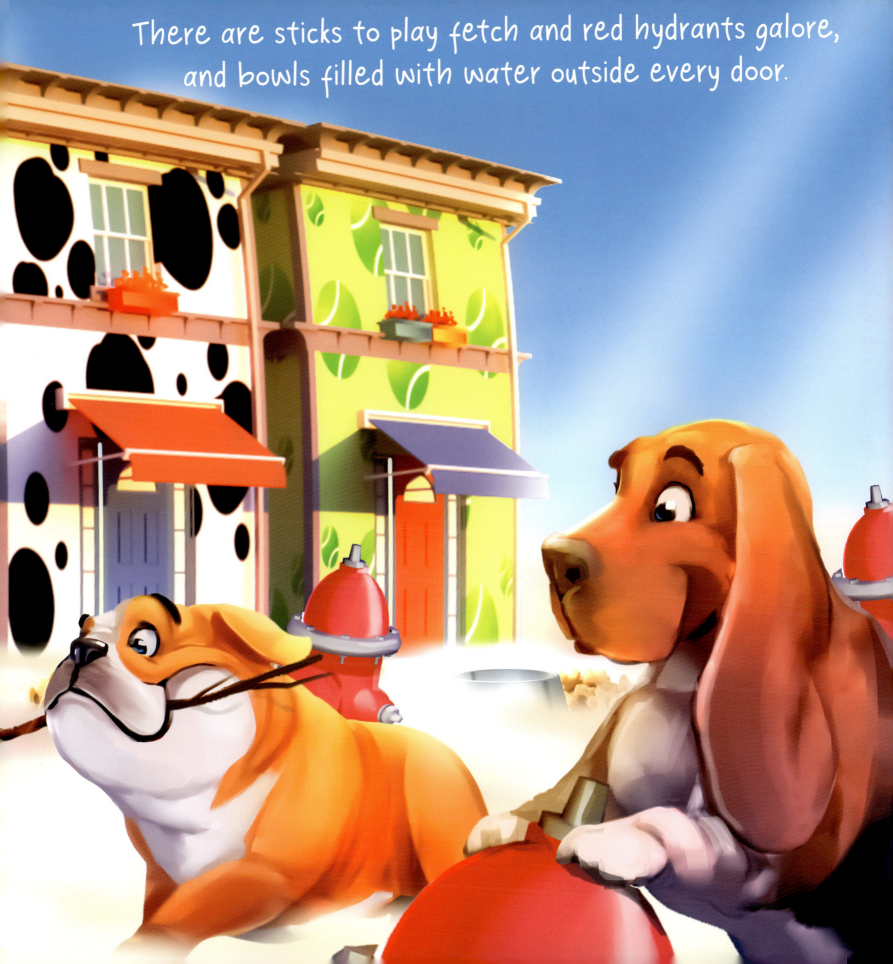

There are sticks to play fetch and red hydrants galore, and bowls filled with water outside every door.

At the end of each day, after hours of fun,
I drift off to sleep knowing you were the one.

There will soon be a day when you're older and grown,
and my love, unconditional, you will have known.

I'm grateful for all of your care, my sweet friend,
and I treasure the love you gave without end.

My family, I miss you and want you to know,

I'm doing alright and I love you all so.

Woof! Woof!

Love,
Pal

*"Though they have gone beyond your sight,
they live in you, your guiding light."*

About the Author:

Amy Skala Tischmann is an award-winning children's book author whose passion for writing began as a young girl.

An entrepreneur at heart, Amy's creative outlets include: photography, book-writing, and operating the Little Free Library and The Little Bookshop. Amy feeds her soul by reading to her sons, enjoying nature, and completing her never-ending list of projects. She lives in Aurora, Illinois with her husband and sons.

About the Illustrator:

Eduardo Paj is a recognizable illustrator celebrated for his animated and expressive artwork. His passion for illustration is deeply rooted in his upbringing. His mother, a painter, was a significant influence who nurtured his artistic interests.

Eduardo continues to captivate audiences with his vibrant and heartfelt artwork, enriching the world of children's literature and beyond.

Loved This Book? Discover More!

If you enjoyed *Love, Pal,* you'll love these other heartwarming and imaginative stories from Amy Skala Tischmann!

New Books Coming Soon!

Explore more books, author visits, and special keepsakes at:
📖 www.redbirdspublishing.com
Stay connected for updates, new releases, and behind-the-scenes fun!

Follow along on Instagram: @amyskalatischmannauthor
Thank you for reading! Your support means the world .💛

LOVE OUR BOOKS? PLEASE CONSIDER LEAVING US AN AMAZON REVIEW!

A Love Letter to My Pet: